PENGWEE'S BREATH

By Debbie Nutley
Illustrations by Alexandra Rusu

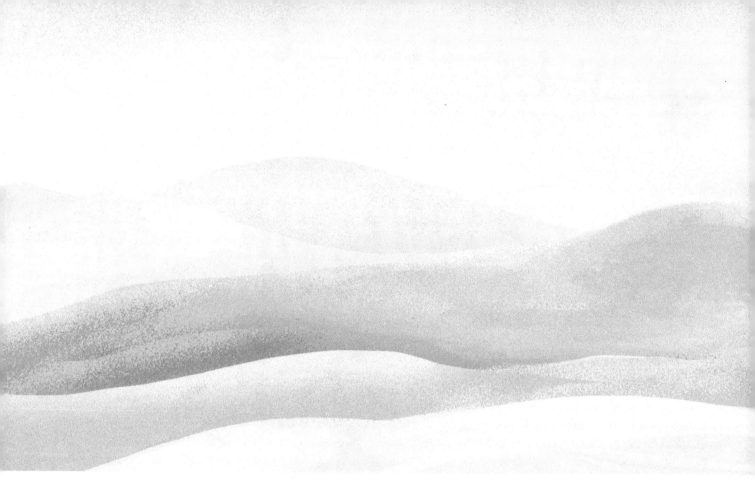

Printed in the United States of America

ISBN 978-1-7377479-0-1 (hardcover)
ISBN 978-1-7377479-1-8 (paperback)
ISBN 978-1-7377479-2-5 (ebook)

Purple Green Press LLC
Chicago, Illinois

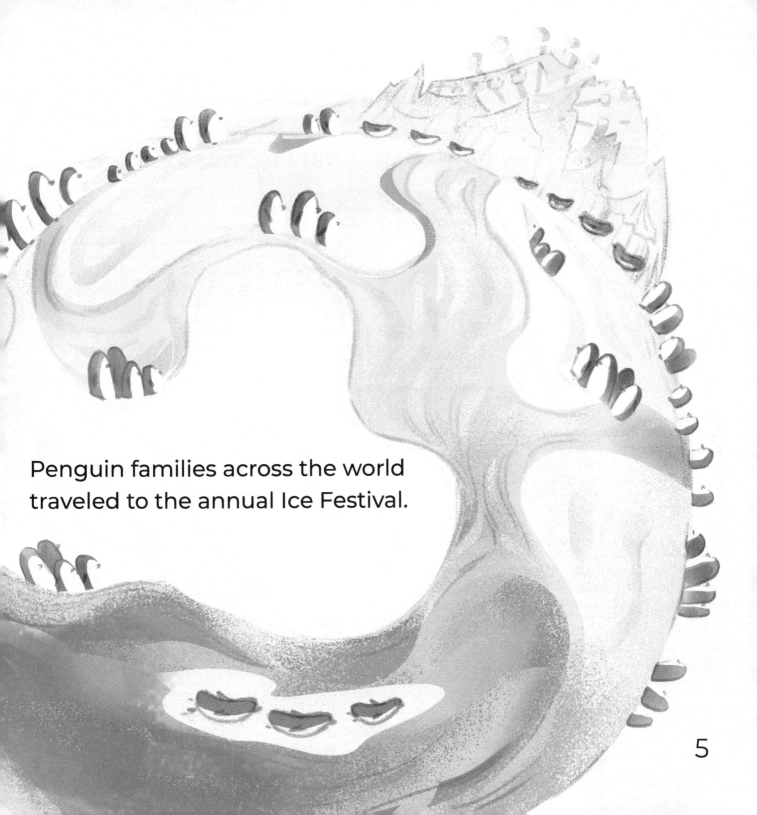

Penguin families across the world
traveled to the annual Ice Festival.

5

Pengwee cleaned his feathers so he'd be ready to go.
He loved everything about
the festival — well, almost everything.

"What rides do you think will be at the Ice Festival?" Mom asked, giving Pengwee a peck.

"I hope they have the Ice Chopper!" Pengwee replied. "But no big scary rides. Just thinking about scary things makes me feel bad — like there's a snowstorm in my tummy and clouds in my head."

"Oh no, Pengwee. Try taking a few deep breaths. It might fight away those snowstorms."

"Like a superpower?" asked Pengwee.

"A Superpower Breath," nodded Mom.

9

Pengwee took in a huge swoosh of air and pushed it out so hard he nearly knocked over his mom!

10

That made them both giggle.

"Maybe a bit gentler," his mom suggested.
"This time, take a big breath in through
your nose. Then slowly, like a gentle breeze,
let it flow out through your mouth."

Pengwee tried it a few times.
He liked the gentle breath,
flowing in, then flowing out.
"I feel warmer inside," said Pengwee.

"I think we're ready for the Festival," said Mom.
As they traveled, Pengwee took big breaths
and imagined he was wearing a superhero cape.

"Just one more hill of snow to climb
and we'll see the Ice Festival!" called Mom.

Pengwee slid down
the hill and saw
his best friend Ruby
waving at him.
Ruby and Pengwee had
played together since they
were little chicks.

Entering the Festival, Pengwee
and Ruby stopped to play Stack the Ice Cubes.

Soon they found
the Ice Chopper,
Pengwee's favorite ride!
They gleefully flapped
their flippers in the air.

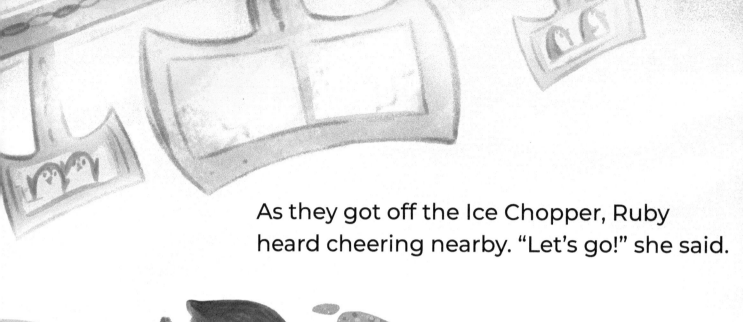

As they got off the Ice Chopper, Ruby
heard cheering nearby. "Let's go!" she said.

Ruby had spotted a ride called the Ice Monster.

The Ice Monster was a frightful beast
with massive claws that could crush a penguin!

"Is this a real monster?" asked Pengwee. But Ruby couldn't hear him. She was already on her way.

Pengwee wanted to catch up but his legs felt wobbly.
He tried not to look at the Ice Monster's crushing claws.
A snowstorm began swirling inside of him.

Pengwee sat down.

He thought about his Superpower Breath and breathed in through his nose, then slowly out through his mouth. The first breath was small, not big like this morning. After a few more tries, his breath got bigger.

Pengwee noticed his tummy and moved his flippers on top. As he breathed in, his tummy went up. As he breathed out, his tummy slowly moved back down.

Soon the snowstorm inside Pengwee began to drift away.

26

Pengwee took one more deep breath and let the air fill his whole body. "Superpower Breath!" he declared and dashed towards Ruby.

As they reached the top of the Ice Monster,
all the penguins screamed with delight.

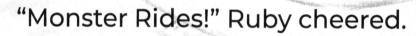

"Monster Rides!" Ruby cheered.

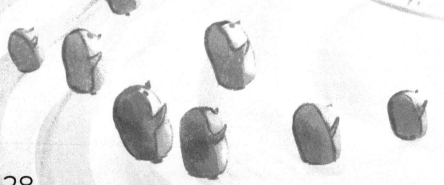

"Let's ride again!" shouted Pengwee.
"There's not a monster in the world
that's mightier than my breath! Or yours!"

About the author

Debbie Nutley is a yogi and writer who loves kids. She began a personal path of yoga and meditation out of curiosity and it soon became a lifestyle. Debbie became a certified meditation instructor and then turned her focus to young minds, becoming trained to teach mindfulness to children.

Debbie has a large extended family with a cadre of kids. They both tire and inspire her. Although her stories include family experiences, names and species are changed to protect the innocent. Eons ago, Debbie's career was in the legal and human resources professions. Then she retired, took a few deep breaths and wrote **Pengwee's Breath**, her debut picture book.

About the illustrator

Alexandra Rusu loves creating vivid worlds and characters from engaging stories and ideas that inspire her. Over time, she's developed a strong personal style where conveying emotions and energy is her main focus. Illustration fills Alexandra with child-like wonder, a feeling she always wishes to keep by her side.

CPSIA information can be obtained
at www.ICGtesting.com
Printed in the USA
LVHW070842190522
719180LV00008B/197

9 781737 747901